First published in Great Britain by HarperCollins Children's Books.
HarperCollins Children's Books is a division of HarperCollins Publishers.

1 2 3 4 5 6 7 8 9

WALT DISNEY PICTURES and WALDEN MEDIA present "THE CHRONICLES OF NARNIA: THE LION, THE WITCH AND THE WARDROBE" based on the book by C.S. LEWIS
A MARK JOHNSON production AN ANDREW ADAMSON film music composed by HARRY GREGSON-WILLIAMS costume designer ISIS MUSSENDEN edited by SIM EVAN-JONES production designer ROGER FORD
director of photography DONALD M. McALPINE, asc, acs co-producer DOUGLAS GRESHAM executive producers ANDREW ADAMSON PERRY MOORE
WALDEN MEDIA SCREENPLAY by ANN PEACOCK AND ANDREW ADAMSON AND CHRISTOPHER MARKUS & STEPHEN McFEELY PRODUCED BY MARK JOHNSON PHILIP STEUER DIRECTED BY ANDREW ADAMSON Walt Disney Pictures

Narnia.com

ISBN 0-00-775992-4

The HarperCollins Children's Books website is www.harpercollinschildrensbooks.co.uk

Printed and bound in Italy.

·The Chronicles of· NARNIA

THE LION, THE WITCH AND THE WARDROBE

WELCOME TO NARNIA

Adapted by Jennifer Frantz

Based on the screenplay by
Ann Peacock and Andrew Adamson and
Christopher Markus & Stephen McFeely

Based on the book by C. S. Lewis

Directed by Andrew Adamson

HarperCollins *Children's Books*

The Pevensie family never dreamed that a magic wardrobe would change their lives!

Lucy was the first Pevensie to find
out the secret inside the wardrobe.

She and her brothers and sister were playing hide-and-seek.
Lucy needed a place to hide!
She dashed inside a wardrobe in an otherwise empty room.

As Lucy moved towards the back of
the wardrobe, she felt a cold wind.
What was going on?

That was when Lucy discovered Narnia –
a magical land full of snow and different,
wonderful creatures!

Later, Lucy shared her discovery.
At first no one believed Lucy's story
about Narnia.

Peter, Susan and Edmund thought she was just playing a game.
How could there be another whole world in the back of a wardrobe?
But soon the other Pevensie children would visit Narnia, too.

Lucy was the youngest in the family.
She loved to read and have adventures.
Lucy also liked to make new friends . . .

. . . like Mr Tumnus, the Faun.
She met him on her first trip to Narnia.

Edmund was the second of the Pevensie
children to visit Narnia.
At first he teased his sister Lucy.
Then he found out her story was true.
But while Lucy made nice friends
when she went to Narnia,
Edmund did not.

You see, Edmund had a way of finding trouble wherever he went.

And that was what he found in Narnia! Just after entering the land beyond the wardrobe, Edmund met the White Witch. She was the evil Queen of Narnia.

The White Witch gave Edmund
some enchanted candy called Turkish Delight.
He quickly fell under her spell.

Peter and Susan, the oldest children, were the last to visit Narnia.

They could not believe their eyes!

At first Susan was worried that her
family might be in danger in Narnia.
She thought it would be safer to go home.

But as time went by,
Susan grew to love Narnia.
She was a fierce protector of Narnia
and its creatures.

Peter, the oldest, always tried to protect his family and keep them together.

Peter tried to protect his family
in Narnia, too.
It was a lot of responsibility,
but as the oldest,
Peter knew it was his job.

The great Aslan saw how Peter took care
of his brother and sisters.
Aslan saw the bravery inside Peter.

He asked Peter to help him lead the creatures
of Narnia against the White Witch.
They worked together and freed Narnia.

The Pevensie family never dreamed
of the adventures they would have . . .

. . . and the many creatures they would meet.

Or that they would later become
Kings and Queens of the magical place
called Narnia!

Peter the Magnificent
Susan the Gentle
Edmund the Just
Lucy the Valiant

Though they returned to their home eventually, Peter, Edmund, Susan and Lucy always kept Narnia in their hearts!